Old Bear

Old Bear

Old Bear and Friends by Jane Hissey in Red Fox

OLD BEAR
LITTLE BEAR'S TROUSERS
LITTLE BEAR LOST
JOLLY TALL
JOLLY SNOW

A Red Fox Book

Published by Random House Children's Books
61-63 Uxbridge Road, London W5 5SA

A division of Random House UK Ltd
London Melbourne Sydney Auckland
Johannesburg and agencies throughout the world

5 7 9 10 8 6

First published in Great Britain by Hutchinson Children's Books 1986
Red Fox edition 1987
This Red Fox edition 1998

Printed in Singapore

RANDOM HOUSE UK Limited Reg. No. 954009

ISBN 0 09 926576 1

Old Bear

JANE HISSEY

RED FOX

IT wasn't anybody's birthday, but Bramwell Brown had a feeling that today was going to be a special day. He was sitting thoughtfully on the windowsill with his friends Duck, Rabbit and Little Bear when he suddenly remembered that someone wasn't there who should be.

A VERY long time ago, he had seen his good friend Old Bear being packed away in a box. Then he was taken up a ladder, through a trap door and into the attic. The children were being too rough with him and he needed somewhere safe to go for a while.

Has he been forgotten, do you think?' Bramwell asked his friends.

'I think he might have been,' said Rabbit.

'Well,' said Little Bear, 'isn't it time he came back down with us? The children are older now and would look after him properly. Let's go and get him!'

'What a marvellous idea!' said Bramwell. 'But how can we rescue him? It's a long way up to the attic and we haven't got a ladder.'

'We could build a tower of bricks,' suggested Little Bear.

Rabbit collected all the bricks and the others set about building the tower. It grew very tall, and Little Bear was just putting on the last brick when the tower began to wobble.

'Look out!' he cried as the whole thing came tumbling down.

'Never mind,' said Bramwell, helping Little Bear to his feet. 'We'll just have to think of something else.'

L ET'S try making *ourselves* into a tower,' said Duck.
'Good idea!' said Bramwell.

Little Bear climbed on top of Rabbit's head and
Rabbit hopped onto Duck's beak. They stretched up
as far as they could, but then Duck opened his beak
to say something, Rabbit wobbled, and they all
collapsed on top of Bramwell.

'Sorry,' said Duck, 'perhaps that wasn't a very
good idea.'

'Not one of your best,' replied Bramwell from
somewhere underneath the heap.

I KNOW!' said Rabbit. 'Let's try bouncing on the bed.'

'Trust you to think of that,' said Bramwell. 'You never can resist a bit of bouncing, especially when it's not allowed.'

Rabbit climbed on to the bed and began to bounce up and down. The others joined him. They bounced higher and higher but *still* they couldn't reach the trap door in the ceiling.

DUCK began to cry. 'Oh dear,' he sobbed. 'What are we going to do now? We'll never be able to rescue Old Bear and he'll be stuck up there getting lonelier and lonelier for ever and ever.'

'We mustn't give up,' said Bramwell firmly. 'Come on, Little Bear, you're good at ideas.'

But Little Bear had already noticed the plant in the corner of the room.

I'VE got it!' he cried. 'I could climb up this plant, swing from the leaves, kick the trap door open and jump in!'

In case it wobbled, Bramwell Brown, Duck and Rabbit steadied the pot. Little Bear bravely climbed up the plant until he reached the very top leaf. He took hold of it and started to swing to and fro, but he swung so hard that the leaf broke and he went crashing down. Luckily, Bramwell Brown was right underneath to catch him in his paws.

'That was a rotten idea,' said Little Bear.

'What I was thinking,' said Duck, 'was that it is a pity I can't fly very well, as I could have been quite a help.'

'Ah ha!' said Bramwell. 'That, my dear Duck, has given me a very good idea. I really think this one might work.'

I N the corner of the playroom was a little wooden
aeroplane with a propeller that went round and
round.

'We could use this plane to get to the trap door,'
said Bramwell. 'Rather dangerous, I know, but quite
honestly I can't bear to think of Old Bear up there
alone for a minute longer.'

'I'll be pilot,' said Rabbit, hopping up and down,
making aeroplane noises.

'And I'll stand on the back and push the trap door
open with my paintbrush,' said Little Bear.

'But how will you get down?' asked Duck.

'I've already thought of that,' said Bramwell, who
hadn't really but quickly did. 'They can
use these handkerchiefs as parachutes
and we'll catch them in a blanket.'

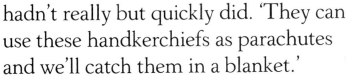

BRAMWELL gave Little Bear two big handkerchiefs and a torch so he could see into the attic. Then he began to wind up the propeller of the plane. Rabbit and Little Bear climbed aboard and Bramwell began the countdown: 'Five! Four! Three! Two! One! ZERO!'

They were off! The plane whizzed along the carpet and flew up into the air.

THE little plane flew beautifully and the first time they passed the trap door Little Bear was able to push the lid open with his paintbrush. Then Rabbit circled the plane again, this time very close to the hole. Little Bear grabbed the edge and with a mighty heave he pulled himself inside.

He got out his torch and looked around. The attic was very dark and quiet; full of boxes, old clothes and dust. He couldn't see Old Bear at all.

'Any bears in here?' he whispered, and stood still to listen.

From somewhere quite near he heard a muffled 'Grrrrr,' followed by, 'Did somebody say something?' Little Bear moved a few things aside and there, propped up against a cardboard box and covered in dust, was Old Bear.

LITTLE Bear jumped up and down with
excitement. 'Old Bear! Old Bear! I've
found Old Bear!' he shouted.

'So you have,' said Old Bear.

'Have you been lonely?' asked Little Bear.

'Quite lonely,' said Old Bear. 'But I've been asleep
a lot of the time.'

'Well,' said Little Bear kindly, 'would you like to
come back to the playroom with us now?'

'That would be lovely,' replied Old Bear. 'But how
will we get down?'

'Don't worry about that,' said Little Bear,
'Bramwell has thought of everything. He's given us
these handkerchiefs to use as parachutes.'

GOOD old Bramwell,' said the old teddy. 'I'm glad he didn't forget me.' Old Bear stood up and shook the dust out of his fur and Little Bear helped him into his parachute. They went over to the hole in the ceiling.

'Ready,' shouted Rabbit.

'Steady,' shouted Duck.

'GO!' shouted Bramwell Brown.

The two bears leapt bravely from the hole in the ceiling. Their handkerchief parachutes opened out and they floated gently down . . . landing safely in the blanket.

W ELCOME home, Old Bear,' said Bramwell
Brown, patting his friend on the back.
The others patted him too, just to make him feel
at home. 'It's nice to have you back,' they said.
'It's nice to *be* back,' replied Old Bear.

THAT night, when all the animals were tucked up in bed, Bramwell thought about the day's adventures and looked at the others.

Rabbit was dreaming exciting dreams about bouncing as high as an aeroplane.

Duck was dreaming that he could really fly and was rescuing bears from all sorts of high places.

Little Bear was dreaming of all the interesting things he had seen in the attic, and Old Bear was dreaming about the good times he would have now he was back with his friends.

'I *knew* it was going to be a special day,' said Bramwell Brown to himself.

Some
bestselling Red Fox
picture books

THE BIG ALFIE AND ANNIE ROSE STORYBOOK
by Shirley Hughes
OLD BEAR
by Jane Hissey
OI! GET OFF OUR TRAIN
by John Burningham
DON'T DO THAT!
by Tony Ross
NOT NOW, BERNARD
by David McKee
ALL JOIN IN
by Quentin Blake
THE WHALES' SONG
by Gary Blythe and Dyan Sheldon
JESUS' CHRISTMAS PARTY
by Nicholas Allan
THE PATCHWORK CAT
by Nicola Bayley and William Mayne
WILLY AND HUGH
by Anthony Browne
THE WINTER HEDGEHOG
by Ann and Reg Cartwright
A DARK, DARK TALE
by Ruth Brown
HARRY, THE DIRTY DOG
by Gene Zion and Margaret Bloy Graham
DR XARGLE'S BOOK OF EARTHLETS
by Jeanne Willis and Tony Ross
WHERE'S THE BABY?
by Pat Hutchins